WATCH OUT!

Ready, Set, Science!
Read all these fabulous, fact-filled, *funny*
MAD SCIENCE® books:

WATCH OUT!

The Daring Disasters of Ethan Flask and Professor von Offel

MAD SCIENCE

by Anne Capeci
Creative development by Gordon Korman

SCHOLASTIC INC.

New York   Toronto   London   Auckland   Sydney
Mexico City   New Delhi   Hong Kong

J
CAp

No part of this publication may be reproduced in whole or in part, or stored in a retrieval system or transmitted in any form or by any means, electronic, mechanical, photocopying, recording, or otherwise, without written permission of the Mad Science Group, 3400 Jean-Talon W., Suite 101, Montreal, Quebec H3R 2E8

ISBN 0-439-20726-6

Library of Congress Cataloging-in-Publication Data available

Copyright © 2000 by The Mad Science Group. All rights reserved.
Published by Scholastic Inc.
Mad Science®: Registered trademark of
the Mad Science Group used under license by Scholastic Inc.

SCHOLASTIC and associated logos are trademarks and/or
registered trademarks of Scholastic Inc.

12 11 10 9 8 7 6 5 4 3 2 1   2 3 4 5 6 7/0
                                              40
Printed in the U.S.A.

1-03
BH

Table of Contents

Prologue

For more than 100 years, the Flasks, the town of Arcana's first family of science, have been methodically, precisely, safely — in other words, *scientifically* — inventing all kinds of things.

For more than 100 years, the von Offels, Arcana's first family of sneaks, have been stealing those inventions.

Where the Flasks are brilliant, rational, and reliable, the von Offels are brilliant, reckless, and ruthless. The nearly fabulous Flasks could have earned themselves a major chapter in the history of science — but at every key moment, there has always seemed to be a von Offel on the scene to "borrow" a science notebook, beat a Flask to the punch on a patent, or booby-trap an important experiment. Just take a look at the Flask family tree and then at the von Offel clan. Coincidence? Or evidence!

Despite being tricked out of fame and fortune by the awful von Offels, the Flasks have doggedly continued their scientific inquiries. The last of the family line, Ethan Flask, is no exception. An outstanding sixth-grade science teacher, he's also conducting studies into animal intelligence and is competing for the Third Millennium Foundation's prestigious Vanguard Teacher Award. Unfortunately, the person who's evaluating Ethan for the award is Professor John von Offel, a.k.a. the original mad scientist, Johannes von Offel.

Von Offel needs a Flask to help him regain the body he lost in an explosive experiment many decades ago. Actually, the professor needs *all* the help he can get. His last miserable experiment in *Mucus Attack! The Icky Investigations of Ethan Flask and Professor von Offel* left him and everything else at Einstein Elementary covered in slime!

But a von Offel embraces disaster before admitting defeat. Maybe the professor can turn Ethan's unit on disaster science into a triumph!

The Nearly Fabulous Flasks

Jedidiah Flask
2nd person to create rubber band

Oliver Flask
Missed appointment to patent new glue because he was mysteriously epoxied to his chair

Augustus Flask
Developed telephone; got a busy signal

Mildred Flask Tachyon
Tranquilizer formula never registered; carriage horses fell asleep en route to patent office

Lane Tachyon
Developed laughing gas; was kept in hysterics while a burglar stole the formula

Percy Flask
Lost notes on cure for common cold in pick-pocketing incident

Archibald Flask
Knocked out cold en route to patent superior baseball bat

Marlow Flask
Runner-up to Adolphus von Offel for Sir Isaac Newton Science Prize

Amaryllis Flask Lepton
Discovered new kind of amoeba; never published findings due to dysentery

Salome Flask Rhombus
Discovered cloud-salting with dry ice; never made it to patent office due to freak downpour

Constance Rhombus Ampère
Lost Marie Curie award to Beatrice O'Door; voted Miss Congeniality

Solomon Ampère
Bionic horse placed in Kentucky Derby after von Offel entry

Norton Flask
Clubbed with an overcooked meat loaf and robbed of prototype microwave oven

Roland Flask
His new high-speed engine was believed to have powered the getaway car that stole his prototype

Margaret Flask Geiger
Name was mysteriously deleted from registration papers for her undetectable correction fluid

Michael Flask
Arrived with gas grill schematic only to find tailgate party outside patent office

Ethan Flask

The Awful von Offels

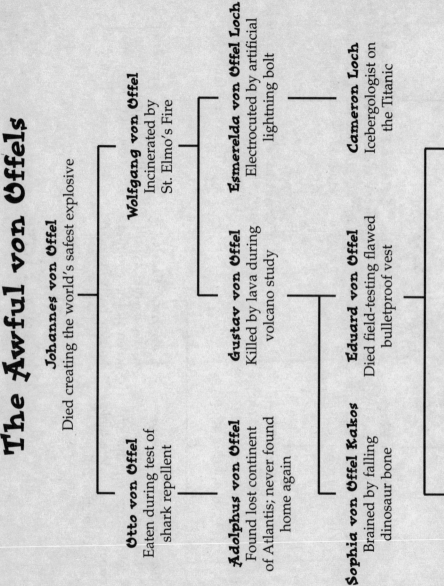

Johannes von Offel
Died creating the world's safest explosive

Wolfgang von Offel
Incinerated by St. Elmo's Fire

Esmerelda von Offel Loch
Electrocuted by artificial lightning bolt

Cameron Loch
Icebergologist on the Titanic

Otto von Offel
Eaten during test of shark repellent

Gustav von Offel
Killed by lava during volcano study

Adolphus von Offel
Found lost continent of Atlantis; never found home again

Eduard von Offel
Died field-testing flawed bulletproof vest

Sophia von Offel Kakos
Brained by falling dinosaur bone

Rula von Offel Malle
Evaporated

Beatrice Malle O'Door
Drowned pursuing the
Loch Ness Monster

Kurt von Offel
Weak batteries in
antigravity backpack

Colin von Offel
Transplanted his brain
into wildebeest

Felicity von Offel Day
Brained by diving bell
during deep-sea
exploration

Alan von Offel
Failed to survive field
test of nonpoisonous
arsenic

Feldspar O'Door
Died of freezer burn
during cryogenics
experiment

Professor John von Offel (?)

Johannes von Offel's
Book of Scientific Observations, 1891

There is a vast power source that many scientists ignore. I must learn to re-create the energy of a natural disaster such as a hurricane or a tidal wave. My early attempts have been disappointing to me and even more so to Jedidiah Flask, who lives next door. My artificial earthquake brought down much of his ceiling. But it was the portable monsoon that really upset him. After all, to see one's chesterfield sofa floating away has to be a shock, especially when one's grandmother is sitting on it at the time.

CHAPTER 1

Cloudy with a Chance of Disaster

Scattered showers. That's what the guy on the weather channel said." Prescott Forrester III squinted through the rain that slammed at him from all directions. "He was sooo wrong!" Prescott shouted so his best friends, Alberta Wong and Luis Antilla, could hear him over the pouring rain. The three of them, hunched under their rain slickers, looked like colorful water bugs darting across the drenched sidewalks of downtown Arcana.

"The worst of it seems to be passing over us now," said Alberta. "But it's not cool to be out in a lightning storm. Let's get out of here." She clutched her backpack underneath her slicker and glanced at the lightning that crackled off in the distance.

Cra-ack!

A jagged bolt of lightning ripped through the sky. It was followed by a clap of thunder that left Prescott glued to the sidewalk with his eyes squeezed shut and his hands clamped over his ears.

Alberta and Luis backtracked and pulled him across the intersection.

"Come on," said Luis. "I know a shortcut that will get us into school and out of this storm fast."

Prescott shivered as a second bolt of lightning cracked. "Why couldn't school be closed today?" he moaned.

"I don't think Einstein Elementary has ever shut down for a *rain day*," said Alberta.

"Besides, lightning isn't some cosmic sign of doom," she added. "It's just static electricity. Like when you rub a balloon and it sticks to your sweater. Still, we shouldn't be out in it. Let's go."

"Static *electricity*? That's supposed to make me feel better?" Water streamed under Prescott's collar as he frowned up at the sky. "Do you guys get the feeling that the lightning is getting even closer?"

"Stay calm, Prescott," said Luis. "Follow me, and let's just keep moving."

Prescott splashed across a river of water that swelled alongside the sidewalk. "Dozens of people get fried by lightning every year. Who can stay calm?" he asked.

Craa-aack! BOOM!

A huge, blinding streak of lightning zigzagged out of the clouds a few blocks away.

All three sixth graders screamed.

"All right. That one was close. Very close,"

Alberta said when she finally opened her eyes. "We should get inside somewhere safe. . . . Hey, what's that?" Alberta gaped at a metal rod sticking up from the roof of their science teacher's old Victorian mansion down the block. "Oh, my gosh. That bolt struck Mr. Flask's lightning rod!"

"A direct hit," Luis agreed. "The metal is smoking, and the air smells burned."

"Nothing to be scared of, eh, Luis?" Prescott said in a shaky voice.

"Well, I know one person who wouldn't be afraid." Luis nodded firmly at their teacher's house. "Mr. Flask. He'd be way too busy checking out the data to be scared."

"Definitely. He'll be psyched that his house was struck by lightning," Alberta agreed. "As long as nothing was damaged."

"Mr. Flask is too smart a scientist to let anything bad happen. I'm sure he took all the right precautions. Not like the von Offels." Luis flicked a thumb at the run-down place that stood next door to their teacher's house.

"With all the reckless experiments that have gone on in there, it's a miracle that old dump is still standing."

The three ran past the burned-out pit where a wing of the von Offel residence had once stood. The rest of the house was in only slightly better condition, marked by broken windows and jagged holes that hinted of explosions. Charred sheets of metal twisted from the roof alongside weedy tufts of grass.

"I guess scientific geniuses like the von Offels don't have time for a lot of home repair," Alberta said.

"You mean, *weirdos* like the von Offels," Luis corrected. "And Professor John von Offel takes the cake. Ever since he showed up at Einstein Elementary, strange stuff has been happening."

"Just because the gym filled up with green slime doesn't mean he's responsible," Alberta said. "You're being totally —"

"Guys!" Prescott raced ahead of his friends. "Can we argue about this when we don't have a gazillion volts of electricity chasing us down the street? Where exactly is that shortcut, anyhow?"

"Okay, okay," said Alberta. Her slicker squeaked as she turned and headed into the park across the street from their teacher's house. "Let's take the shortcut."

"No way," cried Prescott. "Those trees are just begging for the next lightning bolt. We'll be toast!"

"We'll stay in the middle of the field, away from the trees," said Luis. "Besides, the lightning seems to have stopped."

Prescott made no comment. As they marched up the knoll, rain pelted his pale, wet face. His sneakers made sucking sounds with every step he took across the sodden, muddy ground.

"The parks service really should plant some grass seed here," said Luis. "It's like one big mud puddle."

"No kidding." Alberta paused at the top of

the knoll and looked down at the school yard below. "Check it out. The ground is so wet it's actually sagging."

"Which means my sneakers are going to be as wrecked as my mood by the time we get to school," said Prescott. He took another step and sank up to his ankles in a muddy ribbon of earth. "Ugh! Why did I let you guys —"

All of a sudden, the saturated ground beneath him started moving.

"Whoa!" Prescott scrambled to hold on to something.

But there was nothing.

Nothing except a river of mud that oozed toward the school yard. Prescott, Luis, and Alberta went slip-sliding along with it.

CHAPTER 2

World's Laziest Pig

Professor John von Offel ignored the rain that beat against the windows of the sixth-grade science lab. Hands behind his back, he made a slow circle around the fat pink pig that lay on a pile of blankets in front of the lab table.

"Tell me something, Atom," murmured the professor. He turned so he was nose to beak with the parrot perched on his shoulder.

"What is this overgrown pork chop doing here?"

"Awk! Pork chop!" mimicked the parrot.

"You can drop the dumb bird act." The professor shot a quick glance toward the hallway. "There isn't a soul here but us."

"Us and the animal goon squad Flask keeps around for his intelligence study," Atom squawked. He peered at the cages and tanks that lined the walls of the lab. Then he pointed his beak at the pig. "At least Francis here is a lot nicer to me than most of these savages," Atom said.

"This corpulent creature lacks the energy to snore. He certainly hasn't the presence of mind to bother with you," said the professor. He took an ancient, rusted monocle from his pocket and peered through it at the pig. "Francis, you say?"

"Francis Bacon," the parrot answered. "Flask told us about him yesterday. Don't you listen to *anything* Ethan says?"

"The Third Millennium Foundation hired me to evaluate Flask for the Vanguard Teacher Award. I'm not about to suffer through his tiresome prattle about farm animals, too," the professor snapped.

Atom hopped onto the lab table and gazed longingly down at the sleeping pig. "He's got the life," sighed the parrot. "That's how I always pictured my retirement. Nothing but R & R. Poolside, outside my condo in South Beach, Florida. I'm not getting any younger, you know."

"One hundred and thirteen is a respectable middle age for a parrot," the professor answered. "Besides, I need you! I'd see you plucked and batter-fried before I'd allow you to turn into a lump like that," he added, glaring down at the pig. "Come along, Atom. We have important work to do!"

The professor strode across the pile of blankets on which Francis lay sleeping contentedly. Instead of disturbing the blankets, his foot passed right *through* them.

"Better not let anyone else see that," warned Atom. "Those three nosy lab assistants are already on to the fact that you're a ghost."

"Thirty-five percent ghost, not a fraction more," said Professor von Offel. "Yet I must confess, I'm growing impatient. How long must I wait for the day when I will finally be able to cast a shadow or see my reflection? I want to enjoy the comforts of a fully human existence *without* slipping straight through the walls and furniture."

Atom began preening his wing feathers. "Maybe then you'll finally get rid of some of the cobwebs in that wreck you call home," he squawked. "All that dust is enough to choke a bird!"

"You can blame young Flask for that," grumbled the professor. He paced back and forth, with his hands clasped behind his rumpled suit. "He's a Flask! His family has been the source of the von Offels' greatest inspirations ever since I stole the formula for the rubber band from Jedidiah Flask back in 1891. But Ethan is taking far too long. Nothing he's studying or teaching has resulted in anything that has helped me."

The professor scowled at the blank spot on his left hand where his pinkie finger belonged. "It took me 45 minutes to shave this morning. The infernal razor kept passing clear through my skin."

"Look on the bright side," said Atom. "At least you didn't cut yourself."

Ethan Flask was folding his Mylar poncho, complete with Plexiglas hood and windshield wipers, when the principal of Einstein Elementary School caught up to him.

"Do you have a minute, Ethan?" Dr. Kepler asked.

"Absolutely." Ethan slipped the poncho into a pouch no larger than his fist, then fell into step with the principal. "What's on your mind?"

"Well . . ." Dr. Kepler circled around the

custodian, Mr. Klumpp, who was mopping up after the dripping students swarmed to class. "It's about Professor von Offel," she said. "He's had a few weeks to settle in, and yet —"

"He still treats me as if I were a substandard form of algae?" Ethan finished.

Dr. Kepler grimaced. "He *has* been slow to warm up to you."

"To be honest, I'm stumped," said Ethan. "My class has completed some of its finest work ever since the professor has been sitting in. I've done my best to show that science is exciting stuff, an adventure that we can explore a million different ways in our everyday lives."

"There isn't a teacher in the country who's more deserving of the Vanguard Teacher Award than you, Ethan," the principal assured him.

Ethan slipped his hands into the pockets of his lab coat. "I wish Professor von Offel agreed with you," he said. "He takes every opportunity to criticize my teaching methods and my animal intelligence studies. The professor has made it quite clear that he finds me lacking."

Dr. Kepler paused outside the door to her office. "There have been a few — unusual incidents," she said.

"The exploding watermelon," Ethan said, wincing. "And that business of my orangutan mistaking the professor for its mate."

"Not to mention the slime that mysteriously appeared in the gym last week," the principal added.

"It's all so bizarre. It defies explanation!" said Ethan. His eyes sparkled, as if he were contemplating a fascinating scientific puzzle. "Nothing like this ever happened here at Einstein Elementary before the professor arrived."

"And I'd like to make sure nothing like it ever happens again," said Dr. Kepler. "Your future is on the line here, Ethan."

Ethan sighed, rubbing his chin. "Maybe I should have expected this. The von Offels and the Flasks have never gotten along."

The principal shot a stern glance at him. "I refuse to believe a hundred-year-old feud is behind this," she said. "You and Professor von Offel are both accomplished scientists. You never laid eyes on each other before a few weeks ago. Neither of you has even *met* your so-called feuding ancestors."

"Maybe not, but I've heard plenty of stories," Ethan told her. "My father swore it was no accident that our bionic horse placed second in the Kentucky Derby *after* the von Offel's entry. Family lore also has it that Felicity von Offel Day stole the formula for my aunt Margaret's invisible correction fluid — just like her grandfather, Kurt von Offel, snuck away with my great-grandfather's prototype microwave."

Dr. Kepler arched a dubious eyebrow at him. "Those are stories, Ethan," she reminded him. "I should think a scientific mind like yours would require more sufficient evidence than that."

"I suppose I should give the professor the benefit of the doubt," Ethan agreed.

"Quite right. Still, I've been thinking," Dr. Kepler said. "It might not be a bad idea to appeal to the professor's vanity. I don't want him to feel we haven't properly welcomed him to Einstein Elementary."

Ethan nodded thoughtfully. "What do you have in mind?"

"I've scheduled a special board meeting to introduce Professor von Offel to our superintendent and to members of the school board." The principal smiled as she took the attendance sheets from the secretary's desk. "Maybe a bit of fuss and a few compliments will sweeten him up a bit."

"Maybe," said Ethan. "It certainly couldn't hurt."

CHAPTER 3

Human Mud Pies

M r. Flask was halfway down the hall from the sixth-grade lab when he heard laughter burst from the room in loud, giddy waves.

"What in the world —?"

He ran the rest of the way, then stopped short. Three muddy figures stood inside the doorway.

"Alberta? Luis? Prescott?" Mr. Flask said, blinking. "Is that you?"

Thick, gooey mud covered the lab assistants from head to toe. It was plastered to their hair and dripped from their raincoats, their backpacks, and even their noses. The other kids, already helpless with laughter, roared uncontrollably as Francis trotted over and tried to wallow in the puddinglike puddle at their feet.

"It's us, Mr. Flask," Alberta said, wiping her face with a muddy hand. "I know we're late, but" — she pulled a grimy sheet of paper from her backpack and held it up — "at least I did the extra-credit homework."

"We'll worry about the homework later, Alberta. Max, would you get some paper towels?" Mr. Flask said, trying to ignore the scowl Professor von Offel shot at him from his desk at the back of the room. "You three can get the worst of the mud off here and then finish cleaning up in the locker rooms. Now — what happened?"

"We, uh, got caught in a kind of mud slide," Luis explained.

"Kind of? We rolled down that hill like we were a couple of bowling balls!" wailed Prescott. "And that was *after* we nearly got washed away in a flood and zapped by a gazillion bolts of lightning."

"By the way, your lightning rod took a pretty big hit, Mr. Flask. You might want to check it for cracks," Alberta added.

Mr. Flask took the lab assistants' muddy slickers and piled them next to the door while Max Hoof doled out paper towels.

"Lightning, mud slides, floods." Mr. Flask counted off the disasters like a kid listing his favorite birthday presents. "This is marvelous!"

"Try telling that to my mom," said Prescott, frantically wiping his feet. "She just got me these sneakers yesterday."

"Well, science isn't always neat," Mr. Flask told him. "But you three have just experienced something that has fascinated scientists for decades. I'm talking about the incredible raw power of natural disasters like mud slides and thunderstorms," he said.

"You sound like that guy on the all-weather channel," said Sean Baxter. All around him, eyes lit up and students leaned forward.

"Don't forget about hurricanes and tornadoes and tsunamis, Mr. Flask!" Alberta added. "Think of how much force they must have to cause all the damage they do."

"I'd rather not," said Prescott. "Haven't we had enough disasters for one day?"

"Not at all!" Mr. Flask bounded over to the window and followed the rivulets of rain down the glass with his finger. "There's a lot to be learned from storms like this one and from other natural disasters. That's why we're going to start a new unit today: Disaster Science!"

"Cool," said Max.

"Alberta is quite right in her guess that natural disasters pack a lot of power," Mr. Flask went on as his students settled in at their desks and opened their notebooks. "A lightning bolt can heat up to 50,000 degrees in a single second. Tornado winds can reach speeds of more than 300 miles per hour, and earthquakes can wipe out entire neighborhoods in less than a minute."

Luis dropped a sodden wad of paper towels to the floor and grabbed some fresh ones. "We already know a little about mud slides," he said, his mouth curving into a grimy grin. "If that hill was any bigger, the whole school would be under mud right now."

"All the more reason for scientists like us to get the inside story on disasters," Mr. Flask said. "The more we know about them, the better we can predict them and protect ourselves."

"Mr. Flask?" Heather Patterson called, raising her hand. "We're not going inside a *real* tornado, are we?"

"Oh, no," laughed Mr. Flask. "But we are going to do the next best thing — re-create a few natural disasters of our own right here in the lab."

Excited murmurs echoed through the room. Still, Mr. Flask knew there was a chance that

Professor von Offel might not share their enthusiasm.

Say, a one hundred percent chance.

Mr. Flask glanced at the back of the room and blinked in surprise.

For once, there wasn't a trace of disapproval on the professor's face. If anything, Professor von Offel seemed excited. He and Atom stared so intently at each other that it looked almost as if they were communicating some unspoken thought.

Impossible, Mr. Flask realized. Still, maybe the old guy was starting to come around.

"Mr. Flask?"

Mr. Flask shook himself. "Yes, Alberta?"

"Francis fell asleep in the mud. Is that okay? I mean, is it part of your intelligence study?" she asked.

Mr. Flask glanced at Francis, snoring peacefully in the mud at Alberta's feet. "Francis is fine," he said. "I'm assessing his ability to work, not his ability to keep clean."

"Work? That dumb couch potato?" said Sean.

"Sure. Pigs are among the most intelligent land mammals," Mr. Flask explained. "They're even smarter than dogs."

"You mean, that pig is smarter than my cocker spaniel?" Max shook his head firmly back and forth. "No way."

"It's kind of hard to tell," Alberta said. She finished wiping the mud from her hair, then tossed the paper towels into the trash bin. "Francis hasn't done much so far."

"That will change. At least, I hope so," said Mr. Flask. He crouched down to scratch the bristly skin behind the pig's ears. "My theory is that exposure to a school environment where everyone is working will rub off on Francis."

"You mean, he's going to be — studying with us?" asked Heather.

"In his own way," Mr. Flask laughed. "He won't be able to understand the mechanics of disaster science, of course. But I believe being around a group of active, curious students will convince Francis that he should be active, too. We'll see the final payoff when Francis starts to zip around, trying to help us in our work."

"What utter nonsense," Professor von Offel snorted. "That pig wouldn't zip if you put 50,000 volts through him."

"Well, that's another scientific possibility," Mr. Flask admitted. "We'll just have to wait and see which one of us is right, Professor."

"Yes," the professor agreed, glaring through his monocle at Mr. Flask. "We certainly will."

CHAPTER 4

Stress Test

"Prescott! Luis!" Alberta caught up with her friends in the hall before the first bell the next morning. She held her backpack in front of her, with three huge textbooks balanced on top of it.

"I did some research on earthquakes so we'd be prepared for today's lab," she told them. "Here."

Prescott stumbled under the weight of the volume Alberta slid off the top of the pile.

"Open it to the page that's marked," Alberta said.

"A building?" Luis said, looking over Prescott's shoulder.

Alberta nodded. "In San Francisco. They have tons of earthquakes there. Buildings fall down all the time. But this one was designed specifically to stand up to earthqua —"

As she shifted around for a better look, the two other giant volumes slipped from her arms and hit the floor with an earsplitting *thwack*!

Everyone in the hall stopped. Mr. Klumpp's head popped out of the storeroom. His eyes scanned the hall like heat-seeking missiles on the trail of their target.

"It's just us, Mr. Klumpp. Nothing to clean up." Prescott pointed at the fallen books. "I guess our research for disaster science made a kind of disaster of its own."

Mr. Klumpp's eyes blazed. "Nothing scientific about a disaster," he grumbled.

"Sure there is," Alberta said. "Lots of scientists study disasters. You know, earthquakes, hurricanes, tornadoes —"

She didn't get a chance to finish. The custodian covered his ears and went back into his storeroom, shaking his head. As the three lab assistants scrambled to pick up the fallen books, they heard dissatisfied mumbling coming from behind the closed door.

"Not enough that I clean a mountain of mud out of this school without leaving a speck. It'll be a disaster, all right — a disaster for George Klumpp!"

"Disaster science can't be worse to clean up after than our last science unit," Luis said, shrugging. "Mr. Klumpp *burned* his mop after the great mucus spill."

Prescott grabbed the last book from the floor as the bell rang. "Come on, guys."

When they got to the sixth-grade science lab, Mr. Flask was shaking Popsicle sticks from a big plastic bag onto the lab table. "Perhaps you'd like to help set up for today's earthquake experiment, Professor von Offel?" Mr. Flask asked.

"Certainly not." The professor walked to his desk at the back of the room. He set up his inkwell and a small brass perch for Atom.

"I don't know if Atom will need that today, Professor," said Alberta. "He seems more interested in what's going on up front."

The professor scowled at Atom, who stood on the edge of the lab table, staring down enviously at Francis the pig.

"Atom sure seems interested in Francis," Prescott said as he and the other kids sat down. "I wonder why? It's not like Francis is doing anything. He's as sacked out as ever."

Luis took one look at the pig and laughed. "Don't let him out of your sight, Mr. Flask. He looks like he's ready to zip any minute!"

"Francis may be more aware of what's going on than we realize," said Mr. Flask. "And the sooner *we* get to work, the sooner he will. Did everyone do the reading?"

Heather raised her hand. "I didn't get all

that stuff about plate tectonics," she said. "What does that have to do with earthquakes?"

"Excellent question!" Mr. Flask told her. "Who can help Heather out?"

Ten hands shot into the air. Alberta noticed that most of them belonged to boys.

"Luis?" said Mr. Flask.

"Well, the outer layer of the earth is made up of plates that fit together like a puzzle," Luis explained. His cheeks blushed red as he turned to Heather. "When the plates move against each other, they can cause earthquakes."

"Precisely!" Mr. Flask nodded approvingly. "The areas along fault lines — that's where the earth's plates meet — are called earthquake zones. Most earthquakes take place along fault lines."

"Like the San Andreas Fault in California," Heather said.

"Right." Mr. Flask slipped his hands into the pockets of his lab coat and leaned against the experiment table. "Some big cities like San Francisco and Tokyo sit right on fault lines. So constructing buildings in those areas is a tough challenge."

Alberta raised her hand. "The buildings there have to be strong enough to stand up against two different forces, right?" she said. "The force of gravity *and* the side-to-side forces of earthquakes."

"Exactly, Alberta! And that's the challenge you face today." Mr. Flask began sorting the sticks into separate piles. "Working in groups of three, I want you to put together earthquake-proof 'buildings,' structures made of these Popsicle sticks and some Fun-Tak."

"Can we choose our own groups?" asked Sean. He grinned at Heather, who rolled her eyes.

"Fine," said Mr. Flask. "Now settle down and get to work, everyone. We'll test the buildings at the end of class to see how they hold up."

Professor von Offel dipped his quill pen in his inkwell and began scrawling notes in an angular, old-fashioned script. "Seismic energy . . . surely there's a way to use it to my purpose," he murmured.

He picked up his monocle and gazed through it. All around the room, Popsicle-stick structures took shape while students argued and debated.

"Don't make it so tall, Sean," said Heather. "An earthquake will just make it crumble!"

"Who cares?" Sean shot back. "It looks cool like this."

As Sean reached for another Popsicle stick, Atom flew over from the experiment table and landed on the top beam. One whole side of the building collapsed.

"Hey! Atom is interfering, Mr. Flask," Sean complained.

Mr. Flask touched a Popsicle stick left dangling over the gaping hole. "Atom just gave your building a stress test, Sean," he said. "Given the results, I think your group needs to rethink its design."

"I *told* you it was too tall," Heather said.

Mr. Flask, already moving on to the next group, turned back to Heather. "Height is a factor, of course," he said. "But how the building is constructed is important, too."

"Awk!" screeched the parrot. "Too tall!"

Sean glared at Atom.

"Try focusing on your project, not the parrot, Sean," Mr. Flask said.

The science teacher stepped over to Max's group, but Atom flapped over just ahead of him. The parrot pecked at one of the Fun-Tak joints in their building, squawking.

"Parrots can't communicate complex emotions. But Atom does seem to have taken an interest in our work," laughed Mr. Flask. "Max, take another look at that joint. Maybe you can find a better way to anchor the two sides together."

"Over here, Atom!" called Alberta. "I want to test the weight-bearing capabilities of *our* building."

Atom fluttered over to the pyramid-shaped building Alberta was working on with Prescott and Luis. As he landed on the top beam, Prescott stepped back and bit his lip.

"Do you think he understood you?" he asked. "See how he's going from group to group. It's like he's doing it on purpose, to help us test our buildings or something."

"He's a parrot, not an engineer," said Mr. Flask.

The professor frowned as Atom flew to yet another building and began pecking at the Popsicle sticks. "Has he taken leave of his senses?" he mumbled under his breath.

Mr. Flask glanced up from the blue wad of Fun-Tak he was handing to Luis. "Did you say something, Professor?" he asked.

"Nothing that concerns you." The professor got to his feet and walked stiffly over to Atom. He held out his index finger and waited until the parrot jumped onto it.

"I will return shortly," he announced to Mr. Flask. With that, he walked out of the lab.

As soon as he was out of earshot, the professor held Atom up and whispered, "We have work to do. Secrets to steal! Do you have to be so nauseatingly helpful?"

"Pardon me for being interested!" squawked Atom. "Not *all* science involves spying and blowing yourself up, you know. If you'd have concentrated on experiments like these, maybe you wouldn't be sleepwalking through walls today."

"Bah! You'd have made a good Flask," said the professor. "But you're forgetting something, Atom. If I *hadn't* blown myself up, I'd have died a hundred years ago."

Atom picked his way across the back of the professor's collar to his other shoulder. "Your point?" he asked.

"Back off the goody-two-shoes science," said the professor, "remember why we're here!"

"I guess if it will speed up my retirement . . ." Atom yawned, stretching the claws of his feet. "Of course, stealing ideas from Mr. Flask will cut into my relaxation sessions with Francis."

The professor shook his head in disgust. "At this rate, I'll *never* become fully corporeal."

CHAPTER 5

Aftershock

"T ime's up, everyone. Our moment of truth has arrived!" Mr. Flask made a drumroll on top of the lab table and grinned at his class. "Are you all ready to test your buildings?"

"So soon?" Prescott leaned back on his heels and gazed critically at the pyramid-shaped building he, Luis, and Alberta had just finished. "Do you guys think we used enough Fun-Tak? Are the beams strong enough?" He jumped up, measuring the building against himself. "Maybe it's too tall! What if it collapses after all that work we just did?"

"Calm down, Prescott," Alberta said. "Trust me, this building is as strong as anything made of Popsicle sticks could be."

"Definitely," Luis agreed. "We've got cross-beams and diagonal beams. Not to mention crisscross beams along the face of each wall, and gobs of Fun-Tak holding it all together."

Alberta glanced at the professor, who sat at the back of the room while Atom rested on the brass perch in front of him. "I can't wait to see what *he* thinks of it," she whispered.

"Do you really want the opinion of a guy who spends more time talking to a parrot than to other people?" Luis asked, pressing the extra Fun-Tak into a ball and dropping it on his desk.

"Not to mention that he walks through trains in his spare time," Prescott whispered.

"We only saw him do that once, and we're

36

still not sure it really happened," Alberta insisted. "It could have been our imagi—"

The rest of her sentence was drowned out by the loud clatter of marbles rolling across the floor. Mr. Flask, on his knees, slammed down two upside-down cafeteria trays to capture the marbles.

"Got 'em!" Mr. Flask said. He flinched as two marbles rolled right into Francis's snout. "Well, most of them. Sorry about that, Francis."

The sleeping pig didn't move a muscle.

"Oh, yeah. Francis is going to start zipping around any century now," said Luis.

"What's that marble-tray thing for?" Max asked, looking up from the bunkerlike Popsicle-stick structure his group had made.

Mr. Flask rolled the two trays so they were side by side. "These trays are like the tectonic plates that make up the earth's surface," he explained. "Where they come together is like a fault line, where earthquakes typically happen."

"So we put our buildings on the two trays and see how they hold up when the trays move around, right?" Alberta guessed.

Mr. Flask nodded. "Is your group ready, Sean?"

"We were born ready," Sean bragged.

He swaggered over to the rolling trays. Heather and their other partner, Freddy Kirkpatrick, followed, carrying their Popsicle-stick building.

"Set it down so it's on both trays," Mr. Flask instructed. "That's right. Now, I'll just roll these trays a little. Luis, would you count how many seconds the building stays standing?"

"One . . . two . . ."

Crash!

The top of the building collapsed into a heap of Popsicle sticks and Fun-Tak.

"Maybe *you* were ready, Sean. But your building sure wasn't," laughed Max. "It shook right off the foundation!"

"If a building isn't anchored together securely, an earthquake can shake the bottom of it right out from underneath the top," Mr. Flask explained. "That's what happened here."

"I read about that!" Alberta said. "It's called *shear failure*, right, Mr. Flask?"

"Right." Mr. Flask smiled up at her as he swept the pile of fallen sticks off the tray.

Sean glowered at Alberta. "I'd like to see you do any better," he muttered.

"Every group will have a turn," said Mr. Flask. "Let's try the next building."

One by one, the Popsicle-stick buildings were placed on the rolling trays. And one by one, they came tumbling down. Some collapsed from the top, like Sean's. Others twisted around until the entire structure gave way under the stress of the moving "plates." Even Max's squat bunkerlike structure broke to pieces after seven seconds.

"It's our turn now." Alberta gave Prescott and Luis a thumbs-up, then carefully placed their tower on the trays. "Roll 'em, Mr. Flask!"

"One . . . two . . . three . . ." Luis counted.

Prescott held his breath. "So far, so good."

"Seven . . . eight . . . nine . . ."

"Hey! Their building isn't a regular shape. It's a pyramid," Max called out. "Is that allowed, Mr. Flask?"

"Absolutely. Any three-dimensional shape is fine," replied Mr. Flask. "Keep counting, Luis."

"Thirteen . . . fourteen . . . fifteen . . ."

Mr. Flask moved the trays more vigorously. The building swayed and twisted. But after 25 seconds, it still held together.

"We did it!" crowed Alberta, giving Prescott and Luis a high five.

"Excellent work, lab assistants." Mr. Flask gently lifted the Popsicle-stick pyramid from the rolling trays and set it on the ground. "Your design is flexible enough to move with the earthquake, yet strong enough to keep from buckling under the pressure of it."

"That was the plan. I'd love to be humble, but it's pure scientific genius!" Alberta glowed as she turned to the back of the room. "What did *you* think of our building, Professor von Offel?"

The professor didn't appear to have heard her. He was busy frowning at Atom, who stood next to Francis with his eyes half shut, swaying gently back and forth.

"Professor?" Alberta repeated.

The professor blinked. Finally, his eyes focused on Alberta. "Young lady," he said. "In my day, building blocks were used by toddlers, not by serious scientists."

"This from a guy whose great-great-aunt Rula von Offel Malle *evaporated*," Luis whispered, rolling his eyes. "I ask you, is that serious?"

The bell rang, and the professor gathered up his inkwell and quill pen. He stepped right past Mr. Flask, picked up his dozing parrot from the floor, and left without a word.

"Do you want me to help you clean up, Mr. Flask?" Prescott asked, holding back while everyone else grabbed their books and headed for the door.

"That's all right, Prescott. I'll take care of it," said Mr. Flask. He dropped to his hands and knees and rolled the trays to the side of the room. "You go on to your next class."

"Thanks, Mr. Flask. Mr. Santos hates it when we're late for gym. See you tomorrow!" Prescott darted out the door, just missing Mr. Klumpp.

The custodian stormed into the science lab, his jaw clenched and his eyes flashing. "You've done it again, Mr. Flask!"

Mr. Flask looked up in surprise. "Is something wrong, Mr. Klumpp?"

The custodian scowled at the hundreds of Popsicle sticks littering the floor. "Every time I turn around you're at it," he said. "Explosions. Slime. And now this!"

"Sorry about all that," Mr. Flask said. "Don't trouble yourself this time. I'll clean up."

"Now you're trying to get me fired?" Mr. Klumpp's face turned a mottled purple. "No one gets rid of me that easily."

"Mr. Klumpp, please. No one's trying to get you fired." Mr. Flask picked up a few sticks, only to have them snatched from him by the custodian.

Mr. Klumpp charged around the room, picking up Popsicle sticks at a frantic pace until every single one was off the floor.

"Will that be all?" he asked.

Mr. Flask could barely see the custodian behind the mountain of Popsicle sticks in his arms. "Um, yes, Mr. Klumpp. But you really didn't have to —"

"I'll be going then." The custodian turned stiffly toward the door and —

"*Whoooa!*"

His foot landed on one of the rolling trays, sending his legs shooting out from under him.

Wham!

Mr. Klumpp landed flat on his back with a thunderous crash. Popsicle sticks flew through the air, showering down on the custodian, Mr. Flask, and Francis the pig, who continued to snore softly on his bed of blankets.

"Mr. Klumpp! Are you all right?" Mr. Flask ran over, dodging the marbles that were cascading across the floor.

Mr. Klumpp gasped for air as Mr. Flask helped him to sit up. "I'm . . . fine."

"That's a relief." Mr. Flask chuckled as he brushed Popsicle sticks from Mr. Klumpp's shirt. "I'd say that one registered a 10 on the Richter scale, Mr. Klumpp. Total destruction."

CHAPTER 6

Inspiration

Professor von Offel sat in the moth-eaten armchair in his parlor after dinner. In his lap was a copy of *World's Worst Natural Disasters*, a book so dense that it sank halfway through the professor's legs.

"Earthquake, volcano, tidal wave..." He tugged the pages one after another. "It's all wrong!"

A pitted brass lamp cast a yellow light over peeling wallpaper, sheet-covered lumps of furniture, and dusty cobwebs that dangled from the ceiling and windows. With the exception of the professor's armchair, lamp, and a scarred wooden table where Atom reclined on his hammock, the parlor had the look of an abandoned wreck, which in fact it was.

"Bah!" The professor slammed the book shut and dropped it to the floor, sending a cloud of dust balls into the air. "Nothing at all in here that will return me fully to my body."

He thrummed his fingers against the chair arm, then scowled when his fingertips passed through the fabric. "I'm a von Offel! Scientific genius is in my blood!"

He jumped up and walked straight through the wall to a hallway lined with lab tables, dusty glass beakers, and a strange metal cap with wires and metal rods sticking up from it. Rusted metal shelves held a collection of animal parts preserved in formaldehyde: a wildebeest brain, the head of a rhinoceros, fish eyes pickled by the dozen, an octopus tentacle wrapped around a human hand.

"Transspecies organ transplants, brain-boosting electrocution experiments, the development of the antigravity cannonball," he said, pacing back and forth. "Only the von Offels would have had the daring, the *brilliance*, to pull any of this off."

He gazed wistfully at a collection of trophies, certificates, and awards, most of them pitted with acid burns. "I had the genius to bring myself 65 percent back to life," he said. "The rest should be easy! But, alas . . ."

With a sigh, the professor walked back through the wall into the parlor. "The situation is getting critical, Atom," he said. "We must take action!"

The parrot, reclining in his hammock, squawked softly in his sleep.

"Lazy squab," the professor muttered. "You've learned entirely too much from that worthless pig of Flask's."

He grabbed the side of the hammock and sent it spinning.

"Hey!" Atom's startled squawk rang into the dusty air.

The hammock spun wildly between its two poles. Atom was nothing more than a streak of color that twisted first one way, then the other. The hammock held the parrot a spinning prisoner until it finally slowed enough to dump him on the table in a feathered heap.

"What's the idea!" The dazed parrot coughed out a beakful of dust and stumbled up onto his feet. "Did you speed up the earth's rotation again, Johannes?"

The professor stood staring at the hammock with gleaming, inspired eyes. "That's it!" he whispered.

Atom hopped over and pecked at the professor's rumpled sleeve. "Translation, please? I'm not a mind reader, you know."

"Atom, I've finally got it," said the professor. He laughed out loud, his eyes still on the hammock. "Thanks to your infernal napping, I've got the answer!"

CHAPTER 7

Best-dressed Scientist

Nice suit, Mr. Flask!" Luis called out from his locker as Mr. Flask walked into school several days later.

"Thanks," laughed Mr. Flask. "I want to look my best for the crater disasters experiment we'll be doing in today's lab."

Luis's eyes lit up. "Craters? As in, meteorites crashing into —"

"Hi, everyone!" Prescott breezed through the front doors, then stopped in his tracks and stared at Mr. Flask. "Is there a new dress code no one told me about?"

"Nope. Just a meeting with the school board and Superintendent Peters after school," Mr. Flask told him. "By the way, has anyone seen Professor von Offel?"

Luis nodded down the hall. "Alberta and I saw him head into the teachers' lounge a couple of minutes ago."

"Thanks." Mr. Flask's lab coat billowed behind him as he headed for the lounge. "See you in the lab!" he called over his shoulder.

Up ahead, Professor von Offel's unmistakable rumpled form stepped out of the teachers' lounge. The professor held a cardboard coffee container up to Atom, who was perched on his shoulder.

"Drink it," the professor said under his breath. "I don't want you falling asleep on me."

"Professor!" Mr. Flask called.

Professor von Offel lowered the cup of coffee and frowned. "Oh, it's you. What is it, Flask?"

"I just wanted to say how much I'm looking forward to this afternoon's board meeting," Mr. Flask said. "It's quite an honor for the superintendent and school board members to meet a scientist of your stature."

The professor kept walking. "Yes, yes," he mumbled.

"Um —" Mr. Flask eyed the ancient, ratty suit his evaluator wore. "Perhaps you'd like a lift home at lunch so you can change for the meeting?"

"I'm a scientist. I don't concern myself with appearances," the professor snapped. "And I haven't the time to take joyrides in the middle of the day. Good day, Flask."

Coffee sloshed onto his suit jacket as he strode off down the hall.

Mr. Flask was still staring after him when Dr. Kepler stepped from her office.

"Ah! Just the person I was looking for," she told Mr. Flask. "And in a suit, too! I'm sure Professor von Offel will appreciate your extra show of respect at this afternoon's meeting."

"I wouldn't count on it," said Mr. Flask. He smiled and tugged on the sleeve of his suit jacket. "But, hey, if I don't win the Vanguard Teacher Award, there's always the best-dressed scientist award."

"What's with all the flour?" Max dropped his books on his desk as the rest of the sixth graders trickled into the science lab.

"It's for our crater disasters experiment," said Luis. Crouching down, he dumped flour from a huge sack into a half-dozen aluminum trays on the floor.

"We're going to simulate what happens when a meteorite strikes the earth's surface," Alberta added as she and Prescott sorted through a pile of rocks on her desk.

Sean breezed past them on his way to his desk. "You've got to be kidding," he said. "First the earthquakes, then you had us all making tornadoes, now it's meteorites?"

"Meteorites?" Heather repeated, as she

came into the room. Her eyes jumped from one lab assistant to another. "You mean, rocks from outer space?"

"That's right, Heather," replied Mr. Flask. He angled a stepladder into place next to the trays of flour. "I'll bet you didn't know that thousands of asteroid fragments enter the earth's atmosphere every day."

Prescott shot a troubled look out the window. "They do?"

"Don't worry. Most of them are micrometeorites. They're just a tiny fraction of an inch, too small to do any damage," Mr. Flask said. "But every once a decade or so we hear about a larger meteorite smashing a car or crashing through someone's roof."

"They can do a lot more damage than that, right?" said Luis. He set the sack of flour aside and brushed the powder from his hands. "Aren't scientists pretty sure that a big meteorite crash changed life on Earth so much that it may have caused dinosaurs to die out? I mean, weren't there lots of fires and tidal waves and clouds of ash, you know, *disasters*, when that thing hit?"

Mr. Flask nodded, his eyes gleaming. "Scientific data indicate that an asteroid or comet around 10 miles in diameter hit Earth and released energy equal to about 100 million megatons of TNT exploding."

"Wow," said Max.

"Luckily, meteorites that big only come around about once every 100 million years," Mr. Flask said.

Luis raised his hand. "I visited some cousins in Arizona, and they took me to see an enormous hole in the ground called Meteor Crater."

Mr. Flask smiled. "That's one impressive crater — 60 stories deep, and big enough to hold 20 football fields."

"They said the meteorite that hit there was not much bigger than a house," Luis continued. "So why is the hole so gigantic?"

"Great question," Mr. Flask said. He

handed Luis a rock. "Drop this into our flour from about a foot up."

Luis held the rock over the pan of flour and let go. Poof! A soft spray of flour spread out in a circle about a foot wide.

Mr. Flask picked up the rock and climbed the ladder. "When I drop this rock from up here, will it hit the flour with the same force?"

Alberta's hand shot into the air. "No, it'll hit harder. I guess when you drop it from higher, it has more chance to pick up speed."

Mr. Flask dropped the rock. POOF! Flour sprayed as far as Francis's bed. "So you see the effect of more force." The teacher grinned. "Now, consider this: Meteorites hit the ground at about 40,000 miles per hour!"

"Whoa," Sean shouted out. He scrambled out of his chair and grabbed the biggest rock off of Mr. Flask's desk. "Let's see what this baby can do!"

CHAPTER 8

Pow!

Twenty minutes later, the entire science lab was filled with billowing clouds of flour and sneezing students. Several rocks lay half buried in the flour.

Only Professor von Offel seemed unaffected. While everyone else tried to wave the floury dust away, he calmly scratched out notes and diagrams with his quill pen.

"Professor?" Alberta called as she brushed a mound of flour off of Francis. "Should we do something about Atom? He's got a lot of flour on him."

The professor looked up from his notes. He frowned at the white, bird-shaped lump asleep on the blankets next to Francis.

"It's a wonder he's still breathing," he mumbled under his breath. "How is he going to help me like that?"

Alberta exchanged glances with Prescott and Luis. "Professor, what are you talking about?"

Professor von Offel shook himself. "Carry on," he said, with a wave of his hand. "I'll tend to Atom."

He walked to the front of the room as Mr. Flask chose the largest rock from his "meteorite" collection.

"Anyone care to guess what will happen when I throw this rock full force into that last pan of flour?" Mr. Flask asked, climbing with the rock to the very top of the stepladder.

His students leaped back, covering their faces with their hands.

"Good guess," Mr. Flask laughed.

Seeing that all eyes were on their teacher, the professor bent down and brushed the flour from Atom's beak and eyes. "Psst! Atom!" he whispered. "Wake up."

When the bird didn't answer, the professor gently poked Atom.

It did no good. Atom continued to sleep.

Finally, with a snort of frustration, the professor reached out and yanked the parrot's tail.

"Hey!" cried Atom, jolting upright. "What's the big id —"

The parrot blinked, then let out a loud squawk. "Awk! Awk!"

All eyes turned from Mr. Flask to the parrot.

"Atom just *talked*," said Luis.

"Parrots mimic, they don't talk," the professor insisted. He grabbed Atom and brushed the rest of the flour from his feathers. "Now, pay attention to your teacher!"

As soon as Mr. Klumpp pushed his broom around the corner, he saw it: a fine dusting of white powder on the floor outside the science lab.

"Don't tell me," he said.

As he watched, another puff of powder seeped underneath the door and settled in the hall.

"I've had it!" Mr. Klumpp stalked down the hall, holding his broom like a sword in front of him. When he got to the science lab, he gaped at the haze of white that swirled inside.

Mr. Klumpp yanked the door open and ran inside. "Mr. Flask! This time you've gone entirely too f —"

He skidded to a stop as Mr. Flask, on top of the stepladder, flung a rock from high over his head.

Pow!

Flour blasted from the aluminum tray. It flew full force into Mr. Klumpp and mushroomed into a cloud that hid half the room.

Giddy shrieks rang in the air. Students leaped out of the way. And when the dust finally cleared . . .

"Mr. Klumpp!" cried Alberta, brushing flour from her shirt. "Are you all right?"

The custodian didn't move. Flour was plastered over every inch of his face and body, right down to the finger that still pointed at Mr. Flask.

"I'm so sorry, Mr. Klumpp! I didn't see you until it was too late, and then — well, it was too late." Mr. Flask jumped down from the ladder and began dusting off the custodian. "He may be in shock," he called to his students. "Get him some water, Prescott. And see if we can get one of Francis's blankets."

Prescott skidded through the flour toward the sink, while Luis and Max tried to roll the sleeping, flour-covered pig aside and shake out his blankets. Kids tromped flour even farther around the classroom as they ran to help.

"You call this a safe experiment?" Professor

von Offel muttered. "Even my parrot can hardly breathe."

"A little flour never harmed anyone," Mr. Flask said.

"Awk!" squawked Atom. "Can't breathe! Can't breathe!"

The professor glared at Mr. Flask, then picked up Atom and carried him across the flour-covered floor to his desk.

"Pssst!" Alberta nudged Prescott and Luis. "Look at Professor von Offel's feet!" she whispered.

The two boys looked — and their mouths fell open.

"Oh, my gosh," Prescott whispered. "He doesn't leave any footprints!"

CHAPTER 9

No Such Thing

Prescott hovered behind Alberta and Luis outside the science lab after school.

"You guys go ahead," he said. "Three's a crowd, after all. I'll wait out here until you're done talking to Mr. Flask."

"No way. We all saw it. We're *all* going to talk to him," said Luis.

"I can't believe I'm saying this, but Luis is right," Alberta added. "We've seen too much to look the other way. Mr. Flask deserves to know that Professor von Offel is a" — she bit her lip, frowning — "that he could be . . ."

"He's a ghost!" Luis finished.

"A ghost who also happens to be a brilliant scientist," Alberta added.

Prescott rolled his eyes. "Let's get this over with, okay?"

As they went in, Mr. Flask smiled up from the experiment table, where he was working on his laptop computer.

"What's on your minds? A burning scientific question? A new theory about disaster science?" He looked suddenly around the room. "Or maybe you just left your backpacks here in the lab?"

"None of the above," Luis said. He took a deep breath. "Actually, it's about Professor von Offel."

Mr. Flask held up his hands. "Say no more. I know the professor can be critical sometimes, but I really think it's just a question of time before he —"

"It's not about his attitude," Alberta cut in. "It's that, well . . ."

"He's a ghost!" Prescott blurted out.

Mr. Flask blinked. "Come again?"

"I know it sounds crazy, but we've got the scientific evidence to back up our theory," Alberta added.

Their teacher closed his laptop computer and crossed his arms in front of his lab coat. "Maybe you'd better start from the beginning," he said.

He listened while the three sixth graders made their case.

"Hmmm," he said when they were done. "Let me see if I've got this right. You say the professor didn't leave any footprints in the flour this afternoon, and that's why you think he's a ghost."

Prescott nodded. "We saw him walk right into a train once, too. And another time, he just kind of disappeared."

"He tried to tell us our eyes were playing tricks on us," said Alberta, "but —"

"That sounds like a solid, *scientific* assessment," Mr. Flask said. "The professor and I don't always see eye to eye. But I have to say I agree with him on this one. There are no such things as ghosts."

Alberta, Luis, and Prescott looked at one another. "The guy is supernatural. You've got to believe us!" Prescott insisted.

"I'm surprised to hear this kind of superstitious talk," Mr. Flask said. "Especially from my star students. I thought you were scientists."

Alberta looked crestfallen. "We are!"

"Then you should know there's always a rational explanation, even for things that appear to be *ir*rational." Mr. Flask stepped around to the other side of the experiment table, his eyes sweeping the floor. "Take those footsteps, for instance. Dozens of feet crisscrossed the lab floor during our experiment. How many shoe prints would you say there were?"

Luis shrugged. "I don't know. Hundreds."

"That sounds right," Mr. Flask agreed. "How can you possibly remember with any accuracy which ones belonged to which people?"

"But we *watched* Professor von Offel," Alberta said, twisting a strand of hair between her fingers. "He definitely didn't leave any footprints."

"Can you be absolutely sure of that?" Mr. Flask asked.

When they didn't answer right away, he patted Luis on the shoulder. "Don't take it so hard. Your theory shows imagination and creativity," he said. "Those are both important elements of the scientific process. But" — he held up a warning finger — "so is putting our theories to the test."

Prescott looked crestfallen. "So you don't believe us?"

"I believe you mean well," Mr. Flask said. "But let's put this nonsense behind us."

The three lab assistants were halfway to the door when Mr. Flask stopped them.

"Since you're here, I could use some help with one of *my* scientific tests," he said.

The three lab assistants looked at one another and shrugged.

"Sure," said Luis, dropping his backpack to the floor.

"Great." Mr. Flask grabbed a dog leash from a hook on the wall and gave it to him. "An afternoon walk is part of Francis's daily routine, and I've got this board meeting to go to."

"No problem. We'll do it," said Prescott.

A few minutes later, Mr. Flask looked out the window and saw the three of them pulling the reluctant pig across the athletic fields.

Now *there* was a failed experiment, he thought. During the four days Francis had been in class, he had barely moved. Maybe the professor was right, and Francis would *never* zip.

Ethan shook his head as he took off his lab coat and hung it on the coatrack near the animal cages.

"A ghost, of all things," he murmured, chuckling to himself. "How could sensible kids believe it?"

Still, he thought with a frown, *something* was up with Professor von Offel. Not a ghost, certainly. No scientist could ever accept that.

But — how did the representative from the Third Millennium Foundation always land right in the middle of every single crazy, inexplicable thing that happened at Einstein Elementary? And such events had been taking place with alarming frequency lately — starting the very week the professor arrived.

Mr. Flask glanced at the clock above the door. Come to think of it, he wondered, where's the professor now? Our meeting with the school board starts in 15 minutes!

CHAPTER 10

Spin-cycle Science

Atom swooped and twirled among the maze of pipes that twisted through the boiler room of Einstein Elementary.

"Would you mind explaining why we're in the dungeon?" the parrot squawked.

"Centrifugal force!" exclaimed the professor. He looked up from the piles of tools and machine parts on the cement floor in front of him. "The idea came to me the other night when I saw your hammock spinning."

"With me in it," the parrot reminded him. "I still have a headache, you know."

"A small price to pay, Atom. Look!" The professor held up a crumpled sheet of paper covered with formulas and diagrams scrawled out in his old-fashioned script. "I have determined that prolonged exposure to a great amount of centrifugal force will jolt the missing 35 percent of my body to life."

Atom flapped down to land on the floor next to the professor. "That's one serious spin cycle, Johannes. But where are you going to find that much centrifugal force? Wait, I remember. Mr. Flask's disaster science lab, the one between the earthquakes and the meteorites, the one where he had all the kids making —"

"Tornadoes!" parrot and professor exclaimed at the same time.

"Remember when Flask had all those children twirling their little whirlwinds in bottles?" asked the professor.

"Awk!" said Atom. "They made me dizzy."

Professor von Offel reached for a rectangular metal panel and began attaching wires to it. "Well, I'm going to do the same experiment and harness the same centrifugal force, but on a much grander scale, on a *von Offel* scale! This machine will contain all the components necessary to create a Level 10 tornado," he explained. "That's why we're in the basement. These cinder-block walls ought to be strong enough to withstand the high winds."

"You realize you're throwing off my nap time." Atom yawned and began preening his tail feathers. "I'll bet my porcine retirement counselor is sacked out in the lab right now."

"That pork chop is a bad influence on your work ethic," said the professor. "Now, get off my plans. I can't read them."

Atom squawked as the professor yanked

the crinkled sheet of formulas and diagrams right out from under his clawed toes.

"Look who's talking about ethics," Atom screeched. "The only reason you *have* any plans is because you've been taking advantage of Ethan Flask, just like your ancestors have been fleecing Flasks for over a century."

"Where *is* he?" Dr. Kepler whispered to Mr. Flask. "Our meeting was supposed to start five minutes ago!"

The principal shot a nervous glance over her shoulder at the superintendent and members of the school board, who were milling about the conference room.

"Help yourselves to coffee and pastries," she offered, gesturing toward the spread on the table. "Professor von Offel will be here shortly."

Her smile disappeared the moment she turned back to Mr. Flask. "At least, he'd better be," she whispered.

Mr. Flask looked up and down the hallway

for the hundredth time. "I don't know what happened to him," he said. "He's not in his office or in the teachers' lounge. Maybe I'd better make an announcement."

"Just find him — and fast," said Dr. Kepler. "I don't want Superintendent Peters to reconsider our funding for next year's science programs."

"Say no more. I'm on my way!"

Mr. Flask flew through the halls to the office and flicked on the public-address system.

"Would Professor von Offel please come to the sixth-grade science lab?" he said into the microphone. As he spoke, his amplified voice crackled through the hall outside. "Professor von Offel, please come to the science lab."

Professor von Offel barely glanced at the crackling PA speaker mounted on the cinderblock wall of the boiler room.

"It's done!" he cried.

He stepped back from the bizarre cylindrical machine he had just completed. "The

73

moment I've dreamed of for more than a hundred long years is here at last."

"Better late than never." Atom flew in slow circles over the machine, gazing at it with heavy eyes. "You didn't happen to include a napping chamber in that thing, did you?" he asked.

"Bah! Always thinking of yourself," the professor said. "There'll be time enough for sleep *after* I've activated my tornado."

He stepped onto the circular pad at the base of the machine, then pointed to a second pad that was suspended upside down over his head. "These disks will produce a rotating electromagnetic field," he explained, "forcing warm air to rise rapidly over a layer of cool air in a spinning funnel of wind with me at its center."

"I'm getting dizzy already," said Atom. He landed on top of the machine and pecked at a digital meter built into the upper panel. "What's this gizmo?"

"The velocimeter," the professor told him.

"It will record the wind speed of my tornado. I've calculated that 10 minutes of exposure to speeds greater than 300 miles per hour will be sufficient to regenerate the remaining 35 percent of my body."

"You're sure?" Atom bent over the edge of the machine to look the professor in the eye. "You remember what happened when you didn't double-check your calculations for the portable monsoon? Jedidiah's house was underwater for a month!"

"That place needed a good cleaning," the professor muttered. He waved Atom into the air with his four-fingered hand. "Now, stop pestering me and make yourself useful. Turn this thing on!"

CHAPTER 11

Boiler Trouble

Atom spread his wings and fluttered to the ground in front of the machine. With his beak, he pressed the red button built into its base. "Brace yourself, Johannes," he squawked. "It's go time."

The machine hummed and vibrated, filling the boiler room with noise. Slowly, Professor von Offel rose two inches off the bottom panel and began to rotate in the air.

"It works!" he crowed. "I can feel the centrifugal force spinning the life into my cells!"

"You're speeding up." Atom squinted into the wind at the velocimeter. "Already faster than a hundred miles per hour."

Wind sent dust flying through the boiler room. The toolbox blew across the floor and slammed into the cinder blocks. The professor, spinning faster and faster, was nothing more than a blur.

"Yikes!" Atom had to flap his wings full force just to keep his position next to the velocimeter. "Didn't you learn anything from your last tornado?" he screeched. "They made you replant every tree in Wilson Park!"

Mr. Klumpp bent over the heating grill in the cafeteria with some spray cleaner and a rag. "Nothing like a little peace and quiet to get the job done right," he said to himself.

Einstein Elementary gleamed. Dr. Kepler had told him she wanted the place clean for

Superintendent Peters and the school board. So he'd swept and mopped and polished from top to bottom. Even the disaster area Ethan Flask called the science lab sparkled.

No, sir, he thought. They haven't invented a mess yet that got the better of George Klumpp.

The custodian sprayed some cleaner on the heating grill and went to work. But when he went to wipe it with his rag, the cloth was sucked against the grill.

"That's not right," he murmured. He bent close to the grill, testing it with his hand. "The register is *sucking* air instead of blowing it out. Must be something wrong with the boiler."

Mr. Klumpp scrambled to his feet and headed for the basement stairs. As he passed the conference room, he saw Dr. Kepler talking to Superintendent Peters with a nervous smile on her face. Mr. Klumpp hurried past, opened the door to the basement, and started down the stairs.

"You!" The custodian stopped short and scowled at Mr. Flask, who was poking among a pile of discarded desks at the bottom of the stairs. "What are you doing in *my* part of the school? Have you been tampering with the furnace?"

"No, not at all," said Mr. Flask. He opened a metal storage cabinet full of tools and peered into it. "I'm looking for Professor von Offel. Have you seen him?"

"No, but someone's messing with *my* furnace." Mr. Klumpp strode over to the cabinet and pointed to an empty spot on the middle shelf. "And whoever it is took my toolbox!"

Mr. Flask rubbed his chin thoughtfully. "You don't suppose Professor von Offel —"

The custodian was already walking in the direction of the boiler room.

"Wait, Mr. Klumpp!" called Mr. Flask. "I'll go with you."

"Aren't you up to full speed *yet*?" Atom screeched over the howling winds that pinned him to the wall of the boiler room. "I can't move a feather!"

Dust whirled around the spinning professor, pulled from all around the room into the funnel-shaped cloud that stretched between the two disks of the tornado machine.

"Ha!" the professor's triumphant voice came from the center of the cloud. "Just a few more minutes and I shall be fully returned to my body!"

"And *I'll* be squashed like a fly on the wall," squawked Atom. "I'm going to complain to the AARP, the American Association of Retired Parrots!"

"Nonsense! This is the moment of my greatest trium —" The professor broke off in midsentence. "What's happening?" he asked.

Atom peered into the furious winds that ripped at his feathers. "Don't look now, Johannes, but your tornado is *moving*," he squawked. "It's lifting right off the machine!"

"Taking me with it!" cried the professor. "But that's impossible! I calculated that I couldn't possibly detach myself from the pressure poles of the machine. Not unless my spin speed exceeds 600 miles per —"

Even through the raging winds, Atom heard the professor's gasp. "Uh-oh."

"What does the velocimeter say?" screeched the parrot.

"It's whirling out of control. This storm is off the charts!" The professor's wailing voice rose from the whirlwind.

The tornado swept across the floor with Professor von Offel spinning at its center. It passed over Mr. Klumpp's toolbox, sucking hammers and wrenches into the funnel cloud and bouncing them around like Ping-Pong balls.

"Ow!" The professor's head faded away as a T square flew straight through his forehead. "If I weren't already part ghost, that would have killed me!"

The T square bounced wildly through the funnel cloud, then shot toward the wall, driving into it with the full force of the storm.

"It almost *did* kill me," Atom squawked, pulling free a few wing feathers that were pinned to the wall by the T square. "And to think I could have worked for Jedidiah Flask. Just flown out the window, across the alley, and into the next house. So simple! I'd be in my condo in South Beach, Florida, right now, instead of risking my life in another one of your crazy experiments."

"Don't worry," the professor called from the spinning center of the tornado. "Nothing can go wrong — so long as the door stays closed."

At that moment, Mr. Klumpp's voice shouted from just outside the boiler room. "What's going on in there?"

"Uh-oh," mumbled Atom.

Half a second later, the door to the boiler room was pushed wide open.

CHAPTER 12

Runaway Tornado

W hat the —?" Mr. Klumpp squinted into the funnel of dust, wind, and tools that swirled through the boiler room.

"Mr. Klumpp, look out!" Mr. Flask cried, stepping into the room right behind Mr. Klumpp.

A chisel fired from the twisting cloud like a rocket, heading straight for Mr. Klumpp. Before the custodian could move, the chisel snagged the seat of his coverall. It slammed into the cinder blocks right up to the handle, pinning Mr. Klumpp to the wall.

"Hey!" he cried, trying without success to twist free.

"A *tornado*?" Mr. Flask gawked at the funnel-shaped cloud of dust and debris. "But how —?"

Before he could finish his question, the swirling windstorm swept past him and out the door.

"Get me out of here, Flask!" shouted Mr. Klumpp.

But Mr. Flask was already running after the twister. "I'll be back as soon as I can!" he called over his shoulder.

Ahead of him, the tornado picked up desks and metal cabinets. Mr. Flask threw his arms over his head, ducking flying objects. A wave of dread washed over him as he followed a trail of debris up the stairs.

"Oh, no," he groaned. "Not the main part of the school!"

He ran as fast as he could. But when he got to the main floor, the tornado was already halfway down the hall. The roaring twister sucked pens, staplers, chalk, erasers, plants, and textbooks from every classroom it passed.

"Great," groaned Mr. Flask as the twirling mass roared around the corner. "I've found a runaway tornado, but Professor von Offel is still nowhere in sight."

"Come on, Francis," Luis urged. "We're almost there."

He pulled on Francis's leash while Prescott and Alberta pushed the pig down the hall from behind.

"Getting Francis to take a walk is about as possible as getting Heather Patterson to notice me," Prescott said. "Look at him. He's already half asleep!"

"My arms ache from that so-called walk we just took," Alberta added. "The three of us are the only ones who did any walking. Francis just sat there while we dragged him around."

Luis glanced over his shoulder. "Do you guys hear something?" he asked.

"It's probably just Francis snoring," said Prescott. "Let's get him to the lab, okay?"

The three lab assistants grabbed the pig's collar and began pulling him backward down the hall. Francis resisted — until he saw the tornado that whirled around the corner behind them. Then he began to squeal and buck, nearly yanking Luis's arm from its socket.

"Hey, Mr. Flask was right!" cried Prescott. "Francis *can* zip!"

"What's making him go so crazy?" Alberta wondered.

She, Prescott, and Luis turned around — and gaped at the funnel-shaped cloud barreling toward them.

"Hit the deck!" cried Alberta.

CHAPTER 13

A Regular Whirlwind

Alberta, Luis, and Prescott dived for the floor.

"Francis's leash!" shouted Luis.

The leather strap flew from his hand as Francis bolted away from the tornado at lightning speed. The pig's terrified squeals rang through the halls. But they were soon overpowered by the roaring winds of the twister that bore down on the three lab assistants.

For one endless moment, they huddled

together on the floor with their eyes squeezed shut. The tornado howled mercilessly around them. It whipped at their hair and clothes while dust and debris pelted them from all directions.

"Ouch!" yelled Alberta as an eraser bounced off her back.

Then, suddenly, it was gone.

In the eerie quiet that followed, the three dazed sixth graders sat up and dusted themselves off.

"What was *that*?" wondered Prescott.

"I've got a bigger question," said Luis, squinting down the hall after the tornado. "Where did it go?"

"Dr. Kepler, when did you say Professor von Offel would be here?" asked Superintendent Peters.

"I'm sure Mr. Flask and the professor will arrive any minute," the principal told him. "And in the meantime, let me thank you all for taking the time to extend this official welcome to Professor von Offel."

Dr. Kepler cringed when she saw the impatience on the superintendent's face. Members of the school board were growing restless, too. For the past 10 minutes they had been checking their watches.

"I'm sure I don't have to tell you what a tremendous boost it will be for Einstein Elementary if Mr. Flask wins the Vanguard Teacher Award," the principal went on.

"The Third Millennium is the most prestigious science foundation in the country," said the president of the school board. "I'm looking forward to meeting their representative. You don't suppose Professor von Offel and Mr. Flask forgot, do you?"

"Oh, no. Certainly not," Dr. Kepler said right away. "Mr. Flask is completely reliable. And Professor von Offel can be a regular whirlwind when he puts his mind to it."

Swoosh!

Dr. Kepler's mouth dropped open as the spiraling tornado swept through the doorway of the conference room.

"What in the world —?"

Within seconds, the raging funnel cloud tore papers from the table and sucked books from the shelves. Coffee cups and pastries swirled through the air.

"Duck!" cried the school board president. She threw herself under the table, wiping pastry cream from her face. As soon as she vacated her chair, the wind sent it spinning wildly across the conference room and smack into the wall.

"Hey! My hair!" Superintendent Peters made a wild grab with his hand — but not before the tornado snatched his toupee.

The hairpiece spun like a furry Frisbee, sailing out the window on the edge of the funnel cloud. The tornado ripped across the windowsill amid a frenzied clatter of venetian blinds and then disappeared outside.

Several moments passed before Dr. Kepler dared to open her eyes. "Tell me I'm dreaming," she groaned.

But the disaster zone inside the conference

room was very real. The principal, the super-intendent, and members of the school board were up to their elbows in shredded paper, fallen books, and mangled blinds. A layer of coffee and pastry cream covered everything like a wet, sticky skin.

"Ugh!" Superintendent Peters shuddered as he wiped coffee grounds off the bald crown of his head.

"I can explain!" cried Mr. Flask, running into the room. His suit jacket had been ripped half off his body, and his tie flapped over his shoulder. As he jerked to a halt, some bits of chalk and several wing nuts flew from his windswept hair.

"Can you?" The president of the school board frowned in disgust. "Then I, for one, would like to hear it."

"Well, um —" Mr. Flask stared helplessly at the destruction the tornado had left in the conference room. Then he threw up his hands. "Oh, forget it," he said, "I couldn't explain it, not in a million years."

"Excuse me," a shaky voice spoke up from outside the window. "Could somebody give me a hand?"

Mr. Flask ran to the window. He looked out, then blinked at the wild, rumpled form sprawled in the bushes.

"Professor von Offel?" he asked.

The professor's eyes were crossed. His clothes were completely twisted around his scratched, rumpled body. As Mr. Flask hauled him out of the bushes, the professor seemed unable to stop himself from twirling in circles.

"He's spinning like a top," said Superintendent Peters. "Professor von Offel, you must have been caught up in that whirlwind that just came through here."

Dr. Kepler scrambled out from under the conference table and hurried over to the professor. "I'm so very sorry, Professor," she said. "I don't know how —"

"Ha!" the professor cried, still stumbling in circles. His voice vibrated with triumph. "Surely *that* did the job."

He didn't seem at all upset about having been trapped in the tornado, Mr. Flask noticed. In fact, the professor acted jubilant. Still, there was something strange about the whole thing.

"I wonder what caused that tornado?" Mr. Flask stared out the window, then shook himself. "Just a meteorological anomaly, I guess," he decided. "A fluke."

While he tried to hold the spinning professor still, Dr. Kepler took the president of the school board aside.

"Professor von Offel can be eccentric," she said. "But what a brilliant scientific mind! And as you can see, Mr. Flask has an excellent stabilizing influence on him."

"Mr. Flask!" cried Luis. He, Prescott, and Alberta raced into the conference room and screeched to a stop right in front of Mr. Flask.

Luis held up Francis's leash — "we lost your pig!"

CHAPTER 14

Back to the Drawing Board

S low down, Francis," called Mr. Flask.

For the zillionth time since dinner, Francis yanked against his leash, nearly pulling Mr. Flask's arms from their sockets. Mr. Flask had to struggle to keep up with the pig as they made their way down the alley behind his house.

"Go easy, boy," he said.

But he didn't have much hope that the pig would obey. Ever since Mr. Flask had found him — running on the treadmill in the gym — Francis had been bouncing around him like an electron orbiting its nucleus.

Mr. Flask had a strong feeling the tornado had spurred Francis into action, not his exposure to all the work going on in the science lab. And that meant Mr. Flask's theory was down the tubes, all because of yet another bizarre, inexplicable event at Einstein Elementary.

I can't afford to let these weird incidents ruin my work, thought Mr. Flask. And *this* time, I'm going to get to the bottom of it.

He stepped out of the alley into Professor von Offel's backyard. One could hardly call it a lawn, thought Mr. Flask. Unless you counted cannonball fragments, broken-down lawn furniture, and bizarre animal skeletons as landscaping.

Mr. Flask shivered as he passed an ancient deep-sea diving costume that was disturbingly twisted out of shape and punctured with holes. Keeping a firm grip on Francis's leash, he circled around to the front door and knocked on it.

"Professor von Offel?" he called.

The only answer was a loud whirring that reverberated from the other side of the door. The whole house shook with it.

"I know you're in there. I can hear you testing that outboard motor!" Mr. Flask said, raising his voice a notch. "Please come out, Professor. We need to talk about what happened."

"Aren't you *ever* going to stop?" Atom squawked from his perch on top of the parlor lamp. "Your crazy spinning has already burned a hole in the rug."

The professor whirled to a shaky stop, only to launch into another high-speed spin. "Patience, Atom! The residual effects should wear off soon," he said. "What is that infernal banging at the door?"

Atom glanced out the window at Mr. Flask,

who still waited by the door. "You'd better watch yourself, Johannes. That nosy science teacher already thinks you're up to something funny," squawked the parrot.

"Let him speculate," laughed the professor. "Flask will never be able to match my brilliance."

Outside, Mr. Flask finally gave up and walked away, with Francis leaping around him.

"There goes the role model for my golden years," sighed Atom. "Francis is about as restful as a blender now. Thanks to you, Einstein."

The professor twirled to a stop, then shook himself and took a few unsteady steps. "That's it. Time to test the results," he announced.

Professor von Offel pushed his hand against the back of his armchair. It passed straight through the fabric to the other side.

"Oh, well," he shrugged. "Back to the drawing board."

Welcome to the World of
MAD SCIENCE!

The Mad Science Group has been providing live, interactive, exciting science experiences for children throughout the world for more than 12 years. Our goal is to provide children with fun, entertaining, and exciting activities that instill a clearer understanding of what science is really about and how it affects the world around them. Founded in Montreal, Canada, we currently have 125 locations throughout the world.

Our commitment to science education is demonstrated throughout this imaginative series that mixes hilarious fiction with factual information to show how science plays an important role in our daily lives. To add to the learning fun, we've also created exciting, accessible experiment logs so that children can bring the excitement of hands-on science right into their homes.

To discover more about Mad Science and how to bring our interactive science experience to your home or school, check out our website:

http://www.madscience.org

We spark the imagination and curiosity
of children everywhere!